Justin D'Ath grew up on a farm in New Zealand, and he wrote his first book (a ten-page cartoon about his pet turtle, Bubble) when he was nine years old. Since then, Justin has had lots of jobs but has never stopped writing. He now lives in Bendigo and is a full-time author, although he still finds time to teach novel writing to adults and run writing workshops with children in schools.

Justin D'Ath's junior novels are inventive and highly entertaining, full of twisted science, unexpected plots and playful use of language.

www.justindath.com

Other books by Justin D'Ath:

Why Did the Chykkan Cross the Galaxy?
Sniwt
The Upside-down Girl
Koala Fever
Echidna Mania
Astrid Spark, Fixologist

For Older Readers:

Hunters and Warriors

JUSTIN D'ATH

Infamous

ALLEN&UNWIN

This edition published in 2003

Copyright © *Justin D'Ath* 1996

Allen & Unwin
83 Alexander St
Crows Nest NSW 2065
Australia
Phone: (61 2) 8425 0100
Fax: (61 2) 9906 2218
Email: info@allenandunwin.com
Web: www.allenandunwin.com

National Library of Australia
Cataloguing-in-Publication entry:

D'Ath, Justin.

Infamous.

1. Thylacine – Juvenile fiction. 2. Impostors and
imposture – Juvenile fiction. 3. Endangered species –
Juvenile fiction. I. Title.

A823.3

Cover and text design by Sandra Nobes
Cover illustration by Terry Denton
Set in 11 pt Stone Serif by Tou-Can Design
Printed in Australia by McPherson's Printing Group

9 8 7 6 5 4 3 2 1

For Elizabeth Marpole

1 Can you keep a secret?

My name is Tim Chambers and I've got a secret. It's not just the usual kid-type of secret (like, for example, I know who put the dead mouse in the pocket of Mr Gilbert's raincoat) but it's a really big deal, James Bond-type of secret.

If I told my secret I could be famous.

Instead of *infamous*, which is what Greer's mum said I am. I asked her was that the opposite to being famous, and she said not really.

'When you're infamous,' Greer's mum explained, 'you get on TV and in the newspapers the same as famous people do, only you aren't a hero or someone people admire.'

Greer says I'm a hero and someone she admires. Greer is the only other person in the world who knows my secret.

It was her idea that I write this. I didn't want to at first. I said if people read about what really happened, then all the TV people and scientists and the men with traps and guns would come back.

'Not if you write it just for kids,' Greer said. 'Kids are the very best people at keeping secrets.'

I hope she's right. Can you keep a secret?

2 How it all started

It all started with something Greer's mum read in the newspaper.

Greer's mum is Mrs Samson, who runs the only milkbar in Daffodil. I go over there most days after school because Greer and I hang round together. We're not boyfriend and girlfriend, nothing mushy like that. We're just friends. We are both in Grade 5 at Daffodil Primary. In fact we are Grade 5, that's how small the school is.

Sometimes when I go over there Mrs Samson lets us mind the shop while she has a cup of tea and reads the Hobart Mercury newspaper in their kitchen. She and Greer live in a little flat attached to the back of the shop. There's a connecting door that she leaves open so we can

ask her the prices of things if we're not sure.
Usually she talks to us through the open door,
or reads out stuff from the newspaper that she
thinks we might be interested in.

That's how it all started.

It was something Mrs Samson read in the
newspaper that led to my becoming an *infamous
person*.

3 What Greer's mum read

'Hey listen to this,' she said. And she read us an article about how someone down near Rosebery reckoned they had seen a thylacine.

If you don't live around here you mightn't know what a thylacine is. But I'll bet you've heard of the Tasmanian Tiger, right?

Well, it's the same thing. A thylacine is just a fancy name for a Tasmanian Tiger.

For anyone who hasn't seen a picture of one, a thylacine is an animal a lot like a dog, only there are all these black stripes on the back half of its body. That's why the early settlers called them tigers.

They are supposed to be extinct now. The settlers killed just about all of them because they were a danger to their sheep. The last thylacine recorded in the history books died in the Hobart Zoo about sixty years ago.

But every so often you still hear how someone reckons they have seen one. Usually it's late at night on a deserted road somewhere. People used to take those stories seriously, but they don't anymore. Not since I became infamous.

'It's a shame no one ever sees a thylacine round here,' Mrs Samson said after she read out the article to Greer and me. 'It might bring some more people into town.'

Mrs Samson was always trying to think up ways to get more business for her shop.

Daffodil has a population of only twenty-eight people, so she has to rely on outsiders, usually tourists on their way down to Queenstown, to stop and buy stuff in her milkbar. But mostly, the cars zoom straight through town without even slowing down.

'If we had our own thylacine,' Mrs Samson said, 'tourists would flock here hoping to get a glimpse of it.'

4 Elvis with stripes

Have you ever had an idea that just pops into your head out of nowhere?

That's what happened to me while Greer's mother was talking about tourists coming to Daffodil if someone saw a thylacine here. One moment I was listening to what Mrs Samson was saying, then—Pop!—there in my mind was a full colour picture of my dog, Elvis, with stripes on him.

As soon as I could without making them suspect I had a secret plan, I said good-bye to Greer and her mum and ran home. My house is only two houses along from the milkbar, so it didn't take long to get there.

'Elvis!' I called as I went flying in through the gate. 'Where are you, boy?'

Elvis used to be my brother Malcolm's dog before he moved away to Launceston two years ago to become an apprentice baker. Now he's mine—at least I'm the one who has to feed him and look after him.

But I feel funny about saying I own him because in dog years (Dad worked it out) Elvis is ninety-nine. How can an eleven-and-a-half-year-old own a ninety-nine year-old? As I see it, me and Elvis are buddies.

'How would you like to be famous?' I asked Elvis when he came trotting round the corner of the house. I didn't know then that there was such a word as infamous. Elvis didn't either. He just wagged his tail, which meant whatever my plan was, it was OK with him.

5 The plan

Elvis kept wagging his silly tail the whole time I was painting him. This was a pain because it kept flicking me in the face, or else bumping the paintbrush and making the stripes go crooked. But I figured it didn't matter because he would only be in the headlights for about two seconds.

I had already worked out a plan. On the northern edge of town the highway makes a sharp right-hand turn at the vacant block where the old Daffodil Sawmill used to be. At night time, the high beams of every car heading up to Burnie or Devonport swing across that empty paddock like searchlights.

My plan was to get Elvis to stand out there in the long grass where the headlights would light him up. People in the cars would get a two-second glimpse of him as they shot off around the corner.

Two seconds was long enough, I reckoned, for anyone to recognise a thylacine.

6 Civilisation

'It's for Mrs Samson,' I explained to Elvis as
I painted the last bit—the little stripes around
his tail.

'More people will come to buy stuff from her
shop and she and Greer won't have to move
back to civilisation.'

That's what I was really worried about.
If business didn't get any better, the Samsons
might have to leave Daffodil.

Greer had told me her mum owed quite
a bit of money to Mr and Mrs Feldon, who she
bought the milkbar from. If business didn't pick
up, Greer had heard her mum telling Mrs
Gilbert on the phone, she might have to move
back to civilisation.

I hated that word, civilisation.

People went away there and never came back.

First Mum went when I was six, then Malcolm the year before last. Now it looked like my best friend and her mum (who was sort of like a second mum to me) would soon be going there too.

'Will Daffodil ever be civilisation?' I asked Dad before I was old enough to understand what civilisation meant.

'Let's hope not, Timmo,' he said, with one of those laughs that adults make when little kids say dumb things.

Dad is a wildlife officer. He reckons that if Daffodil ever gets to be as big as Burnie or Devonport, a lot of the birds and native animals in the forests around here will be chased away. They might even be killed by pet cats and dogs that people don't look after properly.

That's why we always keep Elvis shut in the yard.

'Pets and wildlife don't mix,' Dad said.

7 Operation Thylacine

Elvis is half Labrador, half red cattle dog. He's brown, but a much darker shade of brown than the thylacine in the encyclopaedia that I was copying from.

So after I had done the black stripes,
I opened a tin of yellow and painted the rest of him with that.

I worked fast, dodging his swishing tail as best I could. It was nearly six o'clock when I finished.

I reckoned I had about an hour and a bit to put my plan into action and then get Elvis cleaned up before Dad got home. He was doing a wombat census near Mount Murchison that week, which meant he didn't get home till after seven o'clock most nights.

I tested out the effect of Elvis' disguise by going across to the other side of the yard and shining a torch on him.

He looked awesome, exactly like a thylacine. Even though I knew it was only old Elvis, a little shiver, almost like fear, ran down my spine.

'Come on, tiger,' I said, opening the gate and leading him out into the back-lane. 'It's time to put Operation Thylacine into action.'

8 A two-kid job

I hadn't counted on it being dinner time.

On an average evening, about two hundred cars passed through Daffodil, heading north. That's about one car every two or three minutes.

But between five-thirty and seven o'clock, almost everybody was having dinner. When it was dinner time, people weren't driving anywhere, they were stopped somewhere, eating.

Elvis and I waited nearly half an hour in the old sawmill yard before I heard the first car coming through the town towards us.

'Elvis,' I called from my hiding place behind a stack of old, mossy timber. 'Come here boy!'

I had made him sit next to another stack of

wood about thirty metres away. My idea was to call him when a car was coming so the people inside it would- see him trotting between the stacks of timber as they went past.

But when the car headlights swept across the open space between the two timber stacks, there was no thylacine to be seen.

Where was Elvis?

As soon as the car had gone, I ran across to the other stack. There he was, exactly where I'd left him, lying fast asleep on the ground.

'Wake up,' I said, shaking him.

He raised his head and licked my hand a couple of times.

'You're meant to stay awake,' I told him.

Elvis yawned.

At that moment I heard another car coming.

'This time get it right Elvis,' I warned him.

I made him stand up and then quickly ran back to my position behind the other stack of timber.

At exactly the right moment, I called Elvis again. But the same thing happened. The headlights flashed across the open space and the only things they lit up were a couple of clumps of weed and a Mars Bar wrapper that must have fallen out of my pocket.

I picked up the wrapper on my way back across to the other stack. When I got there I shone my torch on Elvis. Sure enough, he had fallen asleep again.

Poor old mutt, I thought. When you're ninety-nine it must be pretty hard to stay awake. That was when I realised I was going to need help to put Operation Thylacine into action.

Obviously it was a 'two-kid job'.

9 Wild animals should be left in peace

Dad came home while I was in the middle of drying Elvis off with an old hair-dryer Mum left behind when she went away.

'That looks industrious,' Dad said, standing in the bathroom with a big dopey grin on his face.

Luckily I had let the water out of the bath before he got home. It had been a pretty weird colour.

'He needed a wash,' I said. Which was true, after all.

'Don't take too long,' Dad said. 'I got us some fish and chips at Rosebery.'

Suddenly I decided that Elvis was dry enough. Fish and chips were my very favourite meal. Normally we only had them when we were on holiday.

I turned the dryer off and followed Dad through to the kitchen. Elvis was right behind me; he could smell them too.

'Dad?' I said, as he unwrapped the golden pile of chips and fish and set it in the middle of the table. 'Do you think there are any thylacines left?'

'Probably not,' he said.

'But Greer's mum read in the paper that someone saw one near Rosebery.'

Dad helped himself to a chip and tossed another one to Elvis who was sitting under the chair that used to be Malcolm's.

'If there are any left,' he said, 'I hope no-one ever finds out where they are.'

'Why?' I asked, surprised.

'Because they are wild animals,' Dad said. 'And wild animals should be left in peace.'

10 Not fractions, distractions

Next morning during Maths, I passed Greer a note. **What are you doing tonight?**

She scribbled something underneath and passed it back. *Sleeping.*

Ha ha! I wrote.

I mean between six and seven.

Watching Neighbours.

I need you to help me with something.

What is it?

I'll tell you at recess.

'Timothy Chambers!' Mr Gilbert said loudly from the front of the classroom. 'Kindly bring that to me.'

I stuffed the note into the sleeve of my jumper and took my maths exercise book up to his desk.

'I'm having a bit of trouble with fractions, sir.'

Mr Gilbert didn't even look at my exercise book. 'Not fractions, he said, 'distractions.'

He held out his hand. 'The note please, Tim.'

'What note, sir?' I said.

I should have known better than to try and fool him. Mr Gilbert has got X-ray eyes. Some kids reckon he can even see inside your brain and read what you're thinking.

'The one in your sleeve,' he said.

I felt my face go all hot. With a trembling hand, I gave him the note. He spent the next few moments reading what Greer and I had written to each other.

'So, Tim. Would you like to tell the whole class what you and Greer are going to be doing tonight between six and seven?'

Someone near the front, where the little kids sit, began to giggle.

'No sir,' I said.

'In that case,' said Mr Gilbert, screwing up the note and dropping it into his rubbish bin, 'would you kindly tell the class what you and Greer will be doing during recess.'

I shrugged. 'Probably detention.'

'Exactly right,' Mr Gilbert said with a big smile.

11 Meet me outside the Bat Cave

'This had better be worth it,' Greer said, after everyone else had gone outside for recess.

'It is worth it,' I said.

She waited. I multiplied 6 by 9 and wrote down 54. Mr Gilbert had set us an extra Maths sheet to do so we wouldn't be bored during our detention.

'Well, tell me!' Greer said, nibbling the end of her pen. 'What is it that you want me to help you with?'

'We're not meant to be talking,' I reminded her.

'If you don't tell me now,' she said crossly, 'I won't help you with whatever it is.'

I leaned towards her and whispered: 'Meet me outside the Bat Cave at quarter past six tonight.'

'Not if you don't tell me why.'

'Make sure you wear dark coloured clothes,' I said.

She squinched up her eyes. 'What difference does it make what coloured clothes I wear?'

'Dark colours suit you,' I said.

Greer smirked and went bright pink. She pretends she doesn't like it when I say stuff like that, but I know she does.

12 A little zebra

There weren't really bats in the Bat Cave.
In fact, it wasn't even a cave. It was an old gold
mine that got closed down about a hundred
years ago. It went straight into the side of the
hill behind the Daffodil Hall.

Hardly anyone knew it was there because
it was just inside the edge of the forest that
surrounded the town. A fence had been put
up across the entrance to keep people out, but
Greer and I knew how to get in through a gap
in the wire.

We had never gone in past the first bend
in the tunnel, which was about ten metres in,
but we had made ourselves a sort of cubby
right at the entrance.

That night, when I got there, Greer was waiting for me just outside the wire.

'Sorry I'm late,' I said. I had had trouble with Elvis' wagging tail again. He had knocked over the tin of yellow paint and then it had taken me nearly fifteen minutes to clean up the mess on the floor of the shed.

Greer shone her torch on Elvis.

'What on earth is that?' she asked.

I told her my plan. But instead of telling me how brilliant I was, like I expected her to, Greer said: 'That's the dumbest idea I've ever heard.'

I was surprised by her reaction. And a little hurt, too. 'I'm doing it for you and your mum,' I said. 'So you won't have to leave Daffodil.'

'I think Mum wants to leave anyway,' Greer said.

'What do you mean?' I asked.

'She's lonely since Dad died. All her friends are in Hobart.'

I thought about that. It hadn't really occurred to me before that grown-ups got lonely. For the first time I wondered if Dad felt lonely after Mum left. The only company he had most days, apart from me and Elvis, were the animals he worked with.

I said: 'If lots of people come here to see the

thylacine she might make new friends.' And Dad might too, I thought.

Greer patted Elvis on the head. 'He doesn't look like a thylacine; he looks more like a little zebra.'

'The yellow paint got spilled,' I explained. 'I had to use white to make the black stripes show up.'

Elvis walked over to the wire at the mine entrance and sniffed the air. The fur went up all along his back and he growled.

'At least he sounds like a thylacine,' Greer said with a little laugh.

'He looks like one too,' I said, 'from a distance.'

Greer was still laughing. 'This is the dumbest idea you've ever had, Tim Chambers!'

'You won't laugh when Elvis is famous,' I told her.

As we crossed the road to the old sawmill, I explained to Greer what I wanted her to do. She and Elvis had to hide behind one stack of timber and I would hide behind the other one. Her job was to keep Elvis awake until a car came. Then she had to make him go to me when I called.

'You'd better take his collar off,' Greer

whispered when we got to the first stack of timber.

I hadn't thought of that. It would look pretty silly, I realised, if a thylacine was wearing a collar. I knelt down and undid the buckle.

'Okay, you and Elvis wait here,' I said. I ran across to the other stack. Already I could hear a car coming.

'Tim,' Greer called.

'I know,' I called back. I thought she meant the car. 'Get ready.'

Then I saw her torch flashing around near the other timber stack

'Turn that off!' I hissed. 'They'll see us!'

The car was just coming round the corner near Nixons' garage.

'But Elvis has gone!' cried Greer.

'Where's he gone?' I asked.

'I don't know,' she said. 'He just ran away.'

I darted across the open space between the two stacks. The headlights were getting quite close. I nearly bumped into Greer in the black shadow behind the timber pile.

'You were meant to be holding onto his lead,' I told her.

She didn't say anything, just held Elvis' lead

up close to my face. The opened collar dangled off the end of it.

Now I felt really dumb!

'Which way did he go?' I asked.

'I don't know,' said Greer. 'He just disappeared.'

At that moment there was a loud screech of tyres. Oh no! I thought. Greer and I raced to the end of the stack and peered round it. There, only about thirty metres away, a pair of headlights was stopped in the middle of the road. As we watched, both of us holding our breath, Elvis walked slowly through the blinding glare of the lights and disappeared into the darkness on the other side of the road.

'Uh-oh!' Greer said softly because the driver's door had popped open.

A man stepped out onto the road and stood staring off into the darkness where Elvis had gone. And when the light from inside the car shone on his face we both recognised who it was.

14 Destroy the evidence

I knew I was in trouble as soon as I saw it was Mr Gilbert. Elvis' disguise would probably have fooled just about anyone else but not the principal of Daffodil Primary, with those X-ray eyes of his.

He would have seen straight away that it was just a painted dog. There are only two dogs in Daffodil, and it wouldn't take a genius to work out that the one that crossed in front of Mr Gilbert's car wasn't Mrs Nixon's chihuahua, Sasha.

'What are we going to do?' Greer asked as soon as Mr Gilbert drove away.

'We'd better destroy the evidence,' I said.

Greer grabbed my arm. 'You can't destroy Elvis!' she gasped, sounding shocked.

'Not him!' I said. 'The paint. If we get Elvis cleaned up before anyone else sees him, nobody will be able to prove anything.'

'First we have to find him,' said Greer.

15 Ghosts

He wasn't back home.

It was the first place we tried and where I expected him to be. Both gates were shut, the way Dad and I always left them, but Elvis wasn't in the yard.

'Where do you think he is?' Greer asked.

'I don't know,' I said. Then I had a horrible thought. 'You don't suppose he's been hit by a car?'

'There haven't been any cars since Mr Gilbert,' Greer pointed out.

I felt better then. But not a whole lot better. Dad would go ape if he knew Elvis was out with no-one looking after him. He was always going on about how people should be more responsible about keeping their pets inside their houses or in their yards—especially at night when most of the little native animals came out to feed.

I didn't even want to think about what he'd do if he saw Elvis with stripes.

'We've got to find him and get him washed before Dad gets home!' I said.

We were standing in the dark in the middle of my back yard. Greer flashed her torch around, shining it under bushes and along the line of the side fences. Suddenly the beam stopped on one of Dad's compost heaps. There was a hole like a little cave dug into the pile of lawn-clippings that were pressed up against its wire-netting side. It reminded me of something.

'I think I know where Elvis might be,' I said.

Greer must have been thinking the same thing.

'The Bat Cave!' she said.

We raced back to the Bat Cave and found Elvis sitting just outside the wire looking in. He seemed pleased to see us, wagging his tail and licking me all over the face when I hugged him. Yuk.

Quickly I buckled his collar back around his neck.

'Come on, boy,' I said. 'We've got to get you cleaned up.'

As we led Elvis away through the trees, he kept looking back in the direction of the Bat Cave.

'Do you suppose there's something in there?' Greer whispered.

'Probably ghosts,' I joked.

Neither of us believed in ghosts. But both of us felt a bit spooked from the way Elvis was carrying on. We were glad to get out of the forest and to see the friendly yellow lights of the town all around us.

16 Better than good

What's your favourite day of the week? Mine is Saturday.

But I wasn't looking forward to that particular Saturday because I expected Mr Gilbert would come round first thing in the morning to tell Dad about what he had seen the night before. I knew I couldn't lie about it if Dad asked me.

But Mr Gilbert didn't come round and Dad didn't ask.

Finally someone knocked on our door just after lunch. With my heart thumping like a rabbit in a sack, I went to see who it was. It was only Greer.

'You've got to come!' she whispered excitedly.

'Me and Dad are playing Monopoly,' I said.

'Dad and I are playing Monopoly,' Dad corrected in the background.

Sometimes he's as bad as Mr Gilbert.

Greer made urgent faces at me. Whatever it was she wanted to show me, it must be important.

'Dad,' I called back into the house. 'Can I go with Greer?'

'It means you forfeit the game,' he said smugly.

To forfeit means you lose.

'Okay,' I agreed.

'This had better be good,' I told Greer as I followed her down my front path. 'I just put hotels on Park Lane and Mayfair.'

'It's better than good!' Greer said.

17 What's so funny

The television crew had set up their equipment right in front of the old sawmill yard.

There were two cameras recording the historical moment. One was directed at Mr Gilbert, and the other one was pointed at a lady I recognised from the Channel 6 News.

Mr Gilbert was talking and she was nodding her head in an interested sort of way. All around them were technicians with microphones and clipboards and black boxes with wires coming out of them.

A man speaking into a mobile phone waved at us to stop as Greer and I came barrelling down the footpath.

'That's close enough, kids,' he said.

We stopped where a small crowd had

gathered to watch. Half of Daffodil was there. I asked Kristen Bennet from Grade 3 what was going on.

'They're interviewing Mr Gilbert,' she said.

'We're not blind,' Greer told her. 'Why are they interviewing him?'

'Because he saw a Tasmanian Tiger.'

I'm glad everyone was watching the interview because if they had seen the huge, cheesy grins that spread across Greer's and my faces they would have wondered what was so funny.

18 One hundred percent sure

That night I asked Dad if we could watch the news.

I told him about the interview, so he was interested too. We didn't have long to wait because the story about Mr Gilbert was the very first item on the news.

First there was a shot of the lady interviewer standing outside the old Daffodil sawmill.

'For sixty years scientists have believed that the thylacine is extinct,' she said. 'But in the past week there have been two sightings of the animal in the wilds of Western Tasmania. The first was near Rosebery late on Wednesday night.

'The second occurred last night on the outskirts of the small town of Daffodil. I have

with me the man who made that sighting,
Mr Owen Gilbert, principal of the local school.'

And then Mr Gilbert was on the screen,
saying he had been driving home from the
shop when he saw a thylacine walk right in
front of his car.

'Are you sure it wasn't just a dog?' the
interviewer asked. I squirmed in my chair.

'Look,' I said, to distract Dad from the bit
about the dog, 'there's me and Greer in the
background.'

'Sssssh,' Dad said.

Mr Gilbert was talking again. 'I have very
good eyes.' (I have to agree with that, I
thought.) 'I'm one hundred percent sure it was
a thylacine,' he said.

19 Elvis isn't scared of Thylacines

Later that night Malcolm rang from Devonport. He doesn't ring very often and when he does he usually asks for Dad right away. But this time he didn't.

'Hey little brother,' he said. 'I saw you and your girlfriend on the telly tonight.'

I felt sort of proud that he had seen me on TV. Malcolm was eighteen, a man I guess, and as he'd grown older, he'd stopped taking notice of me.

'Greer isn't my girlfriend!' I said, blushing like a bushfire even though I knew he was just kidding around.

He laughed. 'Do you reckon it really was a thylacine that old X-Ray saw?' my brother asked. Mr Gilbert used to be Malcolm's teacher too.

'Who knows,' I answered.

'You'd better keep Elvis inside at night from now on,' Malcolm warned. 'If he saw a thylacine it might give him a heart attack.'

'Elvis isn't scared of thylacines,' I said.

'Well, just make sure you keep him locked in the back yard at night,' said Malcolm.

I felt sort of guilty then.

20 Civilisation comes to Daffodil

Next day Daffodil was full of people.

All of them had come hoping to catch a glimpse of a real live thylacine. There were tourists and reporters and television crews and even a millionaire who came all the way from Sydney in his own helicopter.

Main Street, where the highway passes through our town, was choked with cars and buses and four-wheel-drives and people driving up and down looking for places to park.

I went to see Greer and found her helping her mother in the milkbar. They were flat out. There were people lined up three-deep at the counter.

'Can you give us a hand, Tim?' Mrs Samson asked.

'Sure,' I said, going round behind the counter to help. What else could I do? After all, I felt responsible for what was happening.

When Dad came looking for me two hours later, Mrs Samson roped him into helping out too!

Even with four of us serving it was hard to keep up with the number of customers arriving.

'We're going to run out of food,' said Dad.

He was right.

By midday all the sandwiches and filled rolls and fruit were gone. We couldn't make more sandwiches because all the bread had been used up or sold already.

People started buying chips and chocolate bars and ice creams for lunch because that was all that was left.

Mrs Samson put an emergency call through to her suppliers in Burnie and in the middle of the afternoon a truck arrived with two hundred loaves of bread.

'Okay,' she said to Greer and me. 'You two can go into the kitchen and start making sandwiches.'

21 One million sandwiches

Do you know how many sandwiches you can make with two hundred loaves of bread?

Neither do I. But it seemed like about a million. All Greer and I did for six whole hours was make sandwiches.

At first we were creative about it. We made meat and cucumber sandwiches, egg and lettuce sandwiches, cheese and tomato sandwiches, salad sandwiches, tuna sandwiches, vegetarian sandwiches, weight-watchers sandwiches, sandwiches for people who can't eat dairy foods, sandwiches for people who can't get enough dairy foods, vegemite and pickle sandwiches, jam and Milo sandwiches, potato chip sandwiches, triple-cheese-and-don't-hold-the-mayonnaise sandwiches, tomato and nutmeg sandwiches, honey, sultanas and pickles sandwiches.

But then we started getting complaints.

When a woman came back saying the mayonnaise in her salami and salad sandwich tasted strange, Greer's mum asked us about it.

'That'll be the caramel ice cream,' I said.

'People are complaining of crunchiness in the mashed egg sandwiches,' Dad reported ten minutes later.

'Hundreds and thousands,' Greer nodded.

'That's it!' Mrs Samson said finally. A man had just brought back one of my 'Hot-dog Specials' (Pal and chilli).

'No more experimental sandwich fillings!'

After that we stuck to the plain stuff. Vegemite sandwiches. Peanut butter sandwiches. Jam sandwiches. Cheese sandwiches. They were a lot easier to make, but much more boring.

'Just think,' Greer said as she slapped raspberry jam on top of the smear of margarine that I had just wiped across a slice of bread. 'If it wasn't for your dumb idea, we could be hanging out down at the Bat Cave this afternoon.'

'Yeah,' I said. But I knew that secretly both of us were pleased about what had happened. Greer's mum wouldn't have to worry about not having enough customers any more.

22 Too much of a good thing

We expected things to slow down towards nightfall. We were wrong. It got busier.

More and more people were arriving in town. Dad said it was because the best time to see a thylacine was at night. Everyone who came into the shop had cameras with flash-lights or torches, or big, battery-powered spot-lights.

'Do you think there really is a thylacine out there?' Greer's mum asked Dad in a rare quiet spell between customers.

'If there is,' he said, 'all the racket these sightseers are making will scare it halfway to Cradle Mountain.'

Finally, at about seven thirty, Mrs Samson closed the milkbar. All the bread had run out and there was not a scrap of food left in the whole shop.

'Whew!' she said, leaning back against the door and mopping her forehead with a tissue. 'What a day.'

I couldn't stop myself from saying: 'You were right, Mrs Samson. You said if someone saw a thylacine in Daffodil it would be good for business.'

'I never dreamed it would be this good,' she said, with a little laugh.

Dad was giving me a funny look but he didn't say anything. He turned to Mrs Samson.

'How would you and Greer like to come back to our place for tea?'

'Thank you very much. That would be lovely,' she smiled.

'What are we going to have, Dad?' I asked as the four of us walked up the busy street towards our place.

He said: 'I was hoping you and Greer might make us some of your excellent sandwiches.'

I looked at him to see if he was joking, but it was too dark to tell.

23 A good cook

Dad was joking.

He cooked up a beef stir-fry and steamed vegetables which we ate in the lounge room in front of the fire.

'You're a good cook,' Mrs Samson told him as Dad was refilling her wine glass.

He actually blushed.

'I don't get much practice these days,' he said. 'With only Tim and I living here, it hardly seems worth preparing fancy meals.'

'That's a shame,' Mrs Samson said. 'I can see Tim really appreciates good cooking.'

I nodded. My mouth was full so I had to wait till I swallowed before I could speak.

'You should taste Dad's hamburgers-with-the-lot,' I said.

24 Endangered species

Next morning during Maths I put up my hand
and asked Mr Gilbert how many stripes the
thylacine had? It worked. Instead of making us
do Sets and Sub-sets, he spent nearly half an
hour talking about endangered species.

25 As quiet as ever

That afternoon I helped in the milkbar again.

Dad came home early (he had finished his wombat count) and helped too. We both stayed till nearly eight o'clock. There was still a lot of tourists (thylacine-spotters, Dad called them) but not quite as many as on Sunday.

Greer's mum was prepared this time. Three truck-loads of supplies had arrived in the morning. As well as sandwiches, we sold pies, pasties and sausage rolls that were kept warm in Mrs Samson's oven.

At one stage I heard Dad say to her, 'You might have to move into the take-away business Clare, if this keeps up.'

'It won't keep up,' Mrs Samson said. 'In a few days everyone will become tired of looking for thylacines and Daffodil will be as quiet as ever.'

26 A wish

By Thursday night it looked as if Mrs Samson was right. We only sold fifteen pies, four pasties and two sausage rolls. Dad and I went home at seven-thirty.

Except for Mrs Nixon out walking Sasha by the streetlight on the other side of the road, the town looked deserted.

'Thank goodness that's over,' Dad said.
We both waved back at Mrs Nixon, who waved to us.

I have to admit that it was nice to have a bit of peace and quiet again. A mopoke was calling softly from somewhere in the forest behind the Post Office. I could hear frogs croaking in Daffodil Creek.

The six left-over sausage rolls in the bag I

was carrying felt nice and warm through my jumper.

'Greer's mum's nice, isn't she Dad?'

'Yes,' was all he said.

At that moment I looked up and saw a falling star. I made a wish.

27 Detention again

Greer passed me a note during Maths. *YOU sneak!*

Why am I a sneak?

You know why!

I don't know what you're talking about.

You could have told me you were going to do it again.

Do WHAT again?

You know what!

I don't know what!!!

You can't fool me!

I was beginning to feel a bit freaked out. What was I supposed to have done? When she had slipped me the last message, Greer had looked really cut.

I picked up my pen and wrote: **Meet me at...**

'Timothy Chambers!' said Mr Gilbert in his sternest voice. 'Kindly bring that note to me!'

28 A real one

I had to wait until lunchtime to learn what was going on and I didn't find out from Greer.

She was in a snit with me and went off with a bunch of girls to shoot baskets on the netball court.

I heard it from Cameron Nixon, who was telling Steve Orton. It turned out I was the very last person in Daffodil to know about it.

'Mum reckons if she didn't have Sasha with her,' Cameron was saying to Steve as I walked past, 'the thylacine would have gone for her.'

I stopped dead in my tracks.

'What thylacine?' I asked.

Cameron and Steve looked round at me.

'The one Mum saw,' said Cameron.

'When?' I asked, a bit puzzled.

'Last night. Sasha scared it off,' added Steve.

'Ha ha!' I said. The idea of Mrs Nixon's chihuahua scaring anything off (except maybe a mouse) was pretty ridiculous.

'It's true,' said Cameron. 'Ask anyone.'

I remembered how Dad and I had seen Mrs. Nixon walking Sasha the night before. I also remembered getting home and being greeted by Elvis just inside the front gate.

'This is a joke, right?' I said.

Cameron shook his head. 'Everyone knows about it. Mum was on the radio news this morning.'

Now I was totally confused. Was someone else painting a dog to look like a thylacine? But why would they do that?

I knew I had to talk to Greer about it.

I ran all the way down to the netball court. But when I got there, Greer turned her back and walked away. Kristen Bennet came over with a message from her.

'She says you're a sneak.'

'Tell her I'm not a sneak,' I said. 'Tell her I truly didn't know what she was talking about.'

Kristen went over and told Greer what I'd said. She came back.

'Greer says if you don't leave her alone she'll tell everyone what you did.'

I knew she wouldn't tell. But I was desperate. Greer was my best friend and the only person I could talk to about what was going on.

'Tell Greer,' I said, 'that it was a real one last night.'

29 What did Mrs Nixon see?

'What do you mean it was real?' Greer whispered.

'It wasn't Elvis,' I said. 'Elvis was home with Dad and me.'

'But they're extinct!' Greer said, loud enough for all the kids on the netball court to hear.

I shrugged. 'If they're extinct, what did Mrs Nixon see last night?' I asked.

30 I almost confess

Greer's mum invited Dad and me to stay for
dinner that night.

It had been quite busy again in the milkbar,
but not as busy as on Sunday. When we closed
the shop, we all went through to the back
where Greer and her mother lived and ate
leftover pies and sausage rolls in front of the
television. The news was on.

Almost straight away there was a report
about how Mrs Nixon had seen a thylacine
crossing the main street of Daffodil at
seven-thirty the previous night.

'It's amazing,' Dad said after Mrs Nixon's
interview. 'Tim and I saw her and Sasha as we
were walking home last night. If we had left

here just a minute or two later we might have seen the thylacine for ourselves.'

'Do you really think there is one, Dad?' I asked.

He looked thoughtful. 'If there was just one sighting,' he said, 'I might have had doubts. But two sightings...well, it seems pretty definite now.'

Dad didn't know about the first sighting—how it had only been Elvis painted to look like a thylacine. I began to feel bad about tricking him.

Maybe I should own up, I thought. Maybe I should tell him and Mrs Samson the truth. After all, what difference would it make now? Mrs Nixon had seen something that wasn't just Elvis with painted-on stripes pretending to be a thylacine so that tourists would keep coming to Daffodil and Mrs Samson would still get lots of customers in her shop.

But just as I was about to own up, another item came on the news. It was something that was going to change all our lives.

31 The $1,000,000 reward

There on the television was the fat cross-looking man who had complained about my 'Hot Dog' sandwiches on Sunday.

Underneath his picture were the words:

**Millionaire offers
million dollar reward**

'Following last night's second sighting of a thylacine in Daffodil,' the newsreader was saying, 'Sydney businessman Athol Fergusson announced today that he will pay $1,000,000 to anyone who can capture the rare animal for his private zoo.'

'Wow,' said Greer. 'A million dollars!'

I started planning out loud. 'We'll dig a pit and put branches over it,' I said excitedly. 'And then we'll get some old smelly meat and...'

Dad was shaking his head. 'Nobody's going to be digging any pits,' he said angrily. 'It's a wild animal. You can't take a wild animal out of its natural habitat and put it into a cage.'

Mrs Samson put her hand on his. 'Perhaps nobody will capture it, Al,' she said.

Mum used to call him Al. Most people call him Allan or, if they're kids, Mr Chambers.

'I hope not,' Dad said. He turned his hand up the other way and clasped Mrs Samson's fingers in his.

32 No thylacine would be dumb Enough to live right in town

It was Saturday morning. Greer and I were sitting in our cubby at the entrance to the Bat Cave. We were listening to all the cars and trucks and four-wheel-drives and helicopters arriving in town. In another half hour we had to go and help in the shop.

'I kind of wish Daffodil was back to how it used to be,' I said.

'It will be', said Greer. 'After they catch the thylacine!'

'Dad said it will probably die in a zoo.'

'Why will it die?' Greer asked.

'Mr Fergusson's got lots of money. He'll give it really good food and a nice kennel to live in.'

'Thylacines don't live in kennels,' I said, 'they live in caves.'

I stopped speaking. Greer and I just looked at each other. I think we both had the same idea at the exact same moment.

'You don't think...?' Greer said, twisting round and looking back into the black tunnel behind us.

I remembered how Elvis had come here the night he had sneaked away from us at the old sawmill. When we came to take him home, he had looked into the cave and growled, as if something was in there. At the time I made a dumb joke about ghosts.

Now a prickly, shivery feeling went running all the way down my back. But, because Greer was staring me in the face, I tried to look brave and unconcerned.

'Don't be ridiculous!' I said. 'No thylacine would be dumb enough to live right in a town.'

'I guess you're right,' she said.

'Of course I'm right.' I stood up and began brushing the dirt off my jeans. 'I'm bored. Let's go down to the shop.'

Greer scrambled to her feet. 'Yeah,' she said. 'They might need us to start early.'

We were both glad to get away from there.

33 Four millionaires

It was a really busy weekend. It seemed like
just about everyone in Tasmania had come to
Daffodil to try to get Mr Fergusson's million
dollar reward. And all of them came to
Mrs Samson's milkbar for food and provisions.

'Word must have got around about Greer's
and Tim's famous sandwiches,' Dad joked with
Mrs Samson at the serving counter.

'Ha ha!' I said from the kitchen where I was
spreading peanut butter and vegemite in stripes
to make our new specialty, *Thylacine Sandwiches*.

Unlike the previous week, we didn't run out
of bread or supplies this time. Mrs Samson had
stocked up as soon as she heard about the
second thylacine sighting.

Three trucks of food had arrived on Friday

afternoon and three more came over the weekend.

By Sunday night all of us were exhausted. For the first time in my life I was actually looking forward to Monday morning, so I could go to school instead of work in the milkbar.

After Mrs Samson closed the shop we all went back to our place for tea.

Dad had Chicken Marengo simmering in the Crock-Pot. It was delicious, as usual.

After tea we all sat round talking about the weekend. Mrs Samson seemed happier than I had ever seen her. Dad was pretty cheerful, too.

'Even if no-one gets Mr Fergusson's reward,' he said, 'there is one person in Daffodil who is going to wind up being a millionaire out of all this.' He was talking about how much money Mrs Samson was making in her shop.

She smiled at him and then at Greer and me. 'Not just one person,' she said. 'Four people.'

34 Families

Next day Greer's mum hired Mrs Nixon's grown-up daughter, Hilary, to work in the shop

This meant Greer and I didn't have to help there after school.

'You deserve a break,' Mrs Samson told us. 'Off you go and play.'

Don't you just hate it how sometimes grown-ups treat you like you're a little kid? *Off you go and play!!!* Grade fivers don't play! We hang out.

Greer and I went and hung out on the Daffodil Oval where Mr Fergusson's helicopter was parked. He had set up his own headquarters in the band rotunda.

A huge sign that said SEARCH CONTROL was strung between two trees.

On the grass behind the band rotunda was a

large wooden box about the size of a garden shed. I pressed my eye up to a crack between two boards but I couldn't see anything inside.

Greer had a look after me. 'It's empty,' she said.

When we asked one of Mr Fergusson's helpers what the box was for, he said it was to put the thylacine in.

'My dad says it's cruel to put wild animals in cages,' I told the man.

'Listen kid,' he said, 'Mr Fergusson loves animals. Do you think he would pay a million dollars for a thylacine if he wasn't going to take care of it?'

'But it doesn't need anyone to take care of it,' I said. 'Nature takes care of it.'

The man laughed. 'If Nature was so good at taking care of thylacines,' he said, 'why is there only a single one left?'

I don't know why nobody worked it out. It was so obvious. You can't have just one of any sort of animal!

The thylacine must have had parents. And even if they were dead, it probably had brothers and sisters. It might even have a mate.

And if it had a mate, I thought, sooner or later they would have babies.

35 One less hunter to worry about

'I'm to blame for all this,' I said to Greer after Mr Fergusson's helper had gone to take two men with tranquilliser guns over to Search Control.

'No you're not,' she said. 'Mrs Nixon saw a **real** one, remember?'

But I still felt guilty. Maybe if Mr Gilbert hadn't seen Elvis with stripes, then there wouldn't have been all this fuss when Mrs Nixon reported what she saw one week later.

'I feel sorry for the thylacine,' I said softly, as we watched more and more hunters arriving.

'Me too,' Greer nodded.

Most of the thylacine hunters had nets to catch it in. Some brought big cages with tricky one-way doors that would let a thylacine in (to get a smelly bone) but not out again. A few used my idea, which was to dig a deep pit in the ground and then dangle a bit of meat over the top so the thylacine would fall in. And the rest had tranquilliser guns that fired hypodermic darts to put the thylacine to sleep.

People who wanted to join the hunt had to go to Search Control to register. When they registered they were given a map that showed the area they were meant to hunt in.

A lot of people didn't like the areas they were allocated (for example: one area was the sewagefarm) and they screwed their maps up and went wherever they liked.

There was a lot of arguing and confusion.

We saw one man lose his temper and throw his big thylacine net right across three of Mr Fergusson's helpers and the big table they were sitting behind.

'I wonder if there's a reward for catching Mr Fergusson's helpers,' Greer joked.

I said the reward was probably a free night in the thylacine crate, which was where Mr Fergusson's two muscly body-guards put the bad tempered man until the police van arrived from Rosebery. The police didn't arrest him but they told him to leave town.

'That's one less hunter to worry about,'
I said.

'One down, eight hundred and sixty two
to go,' said Greer.

That's how many people were officially
trying to capture the thylacine. At Search
Control there was a big whiteboard where the
number of hunters and all the latest news about
the search was written up. There were phones
ringing and people talking into walkie-talkies
and radio microphones.

As Greer and I stood watching, one of the
helpers went to the board and wrote: *Thylacine
footprints found in Sector 238.*

Immediately some television cameramen
jumped into their four-wheel-drives and sped
off towards Sector 238. And so did about twenty
other cars and one helicopter.

'They're never going to catch it making all
that racket,' Greer said quietly.

I looked over at the forest behind the
Daffodil Hall and hoped she was right.

36 Fish and chips

As Greer and I walked back from school the next day we saw a sign on the door of her mum's shop.

CLOSED FOR RENOVATIONS

Several groups of thylacine hunters were standing around on the footpath looking hungry.

'I wonder what's going on?' Greer whispered as we made our way through the groups of hunters. The door was locked so she took out her key and let us in.

'Hi, you two!' said Dad's voice from the back of the shop. He was up on a ladder screwing a big metal chimney thing to the ceiling.

'What are you doing here?' I asked. He was meant to be at work.

'I'm helping Mrs Samson install her new equipment.'

'What's it all for?' Greer asked, looking around at everything.

There were stainless steel benches and pipes and trays and three big shiny troughs with switches and dials on the front.

Dad's tools were scattered all over the place.

'It's called progress,' said Mrs Samson, coming through the door from the kitchen carrying Dad's big electric drill.

'We're moving into fish and chips.'

'Yaaay!' Greer and I both cheered together.

37 A gold mine

Mrs Samson said it was something she should have done a long time ago.

'I should have realised,' she said, selecting a chip from the steaming pile, 'that business was so bad in Daffodil because we didn't serve takeaway.'

'But won't it be the same again when the thylacine hunters have all gone?' Greer asked.

'I don't think so,' she said. 'Now that people know they can get a good feed in Daffodil, they won't break their journey to eat in Burnie or Rosebery or Queenstown. They'll stop here instead. After all, we are right on the main highway.'

I slipped a dim sim under the table to Elvis. 'So you won't be leaving Daffodil now?' I asked.

Dad frowned suddenly and looked sideways at Greer's mum.

'Why on earth would I leave here?' she asked, catching Dad's eye and grinning in a way that made her look a bit like Greer. 'Now that we've moved into take-away, this business of ours looks like turning into a regular gold mine!'

38 Packing death

'What if it attacks us?' Greer whispered.

'It won't,' I said. I shone my torch into the old mine. The dull orange beam only went as far as the first corner, about five metres in front of us. 'Animals can sense it when you don't mean them any harm.'

I wished I was even half as confident as I sounded. Going into the Bat Cave wasn't exactly number one on my list of the ten best ways to spend a Saturday afternoon.

In fact, it wasn't even on the list. I was packing death.

'Anyway,' I said, 'Elvis will look after us.'

I patted him on the back. He growled softly and pulled on his lead. He was the bravest dog in the world, I thought.

There was an old photograph in one of Dad's natural history books that showed a thylacine yawning. Its mouth was open as wide as a crocodile's; and it seemed to have about the same number of teeth.

As Greer, Elvis and I inched our way towards the bend in the tunnel, I had a sudden picture in my mind of an enormous mouth with pointed white teeth exploding out of the darkness, rushing straight at my face like a raptor in *Jurassic Park*.

I just about lost my nerve then. Why were we doing this? I asked myself. There wasn't really an answer, at least not one that made any sense. Maybe it was because the whole of Daffodil had become thylacine mad and I'd finally caught the bug.

I wanted to see the thylacine for myself. To see what a million dollar animal looked like, I guess. And I think I had a crazy notion, somewhere deep inside my head, of making friends, maybe even getting myself a very unusual pet.

It was only afterwards that I realised the stupid risk Greer and I took that Saturday afternoon. But neither of us knew, as we came up to the bend in the tunnel, what to expect as we crept around the corner.

39 Dad figures out something

I'll tell you something I hate. You're reading a book and you have just got to a really exciting bit when suddenly the action switches to a completely different part of the story, one that is probably quite important but not nearly so exciting.

All you want to do is skip over this boring bit and go straight to the next chapter where (for example) two young heroes make their amazing discovery.

But please don't! Or else, read Chapters 41 and 42 and then come back and read Chapter 40. I'll make it as short as possible.

You see, the night before Greer and I made our amazing discovery, Dad figured out something very important.

40 The (not really) boring bit

On Friday morning, as Dad and I were eating
breakfast, a report came over the radio that
there had been a third sighting of the thylacine.

This time it wasn't a local resident who
saw the creature. It was a travelling salesman
who had stopped in Daffodil to buy fish and
chips on his way down to Queenstown.

On the radio news, the travelling salesman
was saying that the thylacine crossed the main
street of Daffodil right in front of him.

'It was bold as brass,' he said, 'as if it lived
right there in the town.'

Dad put down his cup.

'That's it!' he said. 'It must live here!'

I nearly choked on my Weet-bix. 'What do
you mean?' I asked, trying to sound

unconcerned. 'How could it live here without us seeing it every day?'

'They only come out at night,' said Dad.

'But where would it hide in the daytime?' I asked.

'It wouldn't live right in town,' Dad said, 'but somewhere close by. That would explain why Mr Fergusson's men haven't caught it— they've been looking for it out in the forest. But it has been right here under their noses the whole time!'

I wondered whether I should tell him about the Bat Cave.

'The question is,' Dad went on (he was sort of talking to himself like he does when he's trying to figure something out). 'The question is why has it stayed here? Why haven't all the people and cars and helicopters scared it away?'

And then Dad answered his own question. 'Because it has a family!'

41 The thing that saved us

The most dangerous sort of animal, Dad once told me, is a mother protecting its young.

I don't know why I took such a stupid risk. Anything could have happened that Saturday when Greer and I went into the Bat Cave.

The only thing that saved us, I realised later, was Mr Fergusson's one million dollar reward. While Greer, Elvis and I were creeping through the old mine shaft to make *our* amazing discovery, a retired prospector named Nelson Tootell, way up on Mount Daffodil, in Sector 466, who had come all the way from Coober Pedy to capture the famous Daffodil thylacine, was doing a victory dance around a large wooden box-trap. From inside could be heard a series of deep, angry growls.

42 Around the corner

Elvis got to the corner first. Then he suddenly stopped and allowed his lead to go slack. I bumped into him and nearly fell over.

'What's wrong?' Greer whispered.

'Elvis won't go any further,' I told her.

'Let's go back,' she said.

A little voice inside me was saying, 'Yeah, get the hell out of here!' But I didn't want Greer to think I was a wuss.

'I'll just take a look,' I said.

I shuffled up beside Elvis. I didn't know what to expect. Nervously I poked my torch around the bend. Its dim light lit up a small cavern about the size of a room. The ceiling was not much higher than my head and was propped up by thick wooden beams. Moss and spider-webs clung to the rotten wood. Knobbly tree roots poked out of the walls like the claws of buried dinosaurs. I had a creepy feeling that something was watching us. Elvis still hadn't moved.

I shone my torch around the cavern. In one corner was a pile of rubble where one of the roof beams had fallen down.

Under it was a neat little cubby hole just big enough for a medium-sized animal. I shone the torch beam into it. Four little eyes blinked back.

'What is it?' Greer whispered.

I jumped. I hadn't heard her coming up to stand next to me.

'I don't know,' I said. I hoped she wouldn't notice me trembling. 'Something is in there.'

One pair of eyes came forward. Two pointy ears appeared, followed by a tiny, pointy face.

'It's baby animals,' Greer said. 'Puppies!'

Before I could stop her she darted past me into the cavern.

'Don't!' I warned her. But she'd already reached into the gap and pulled out a little bundle of fur.

'Oh, isn't it gorgeous!' she crooned, cuddling the strange-looking creature up against her jumper. It was about the size of a guinea pig, with stubby legs and a long, thin tail.

The stripes were a bit of a let-down, I thought. They were thin and quite pale, not nearly as good as the ones I'd painted on Elvis.

'It's a thylacine,' I said. 'You had better put it back.'

I was worried about the mother. I shone my torch in a circle, expecting her to leap out at any moment. But nothing happened. Elvis was still at the entrance to the cavern. His tail was wagging now so I guessed that meant there wasn't any danger. The mother must be away somewhere. I bent down and lifted the other cub out of its den.

'Can we keep them?' Greer asked.

'Of course not,' I said. 'They're wild animals.'

But part of me wanted to keep them. We would be famous; the only people in the world with thylacines for pets.

'Do you realise you're holding one million dollars?' Greer asked me.

I thought about what I could do with all that money. Dad wouldn't have to work anymore and neither would Greer's mum.

We could all move to Devonport and get a

great big house. There would be enough room for Malcolm to live with us, too, and even a spare room for Mum when she came over from Melbourne to visit.

Dad and Mrs Samson could get married.

Which would mean, I suddenly realised, that Greer would be my sister. I felt kind of funny about that.

'Maybe we could just take one of them,' Greer said.

'No,' I said. 'It would miss its mother too much.'

We both thought about the mother then.

'Where do you think she is?' Greer said, suddenly whispering.

'Probably away getting food,' I whispered back. But then I remembered what Dad had said. 'Usually they only go out at night.'

I shivered. Both of us sensed that something was wrong.

'This place gives me the creeps!' Greer said.

Quickly we put the baby thylacines back inside their cubby. Then I picked up Elvis' lead and we hurried out of the Bat Cave.

43 The fence

'What would you do with a million dollars?'
I asked Dad that afternoon.

He thought about it for a moment. 'I'd build
a two metre fence right along the edge of the
forest,' he said.

'To keep the thylacines in?' I asked.

'To keep people out,' Dad said.

44 Caught!

It was ten o'clock that Saturday night when someone knocked on our door.

Although I had been in bed for half an hour, I was still wide awake. I was lying there thinking about the baby thylacines and how mad I'd be
if someone else found them and took them to Mr Fergusson for the reward. Then I would really be kicking myself for letting the two million dollars slip through my fingers.

I heard Dad opening the door and then I heard him and Greer's mum talking.

'Damn!' I heard Dad say a couple of times. I was surprised because he hardly ever gets upset or uses that kind of language.

I got out of bed and tip-toed into the

passage. I stood in the shadows just outside the kitchen doorway where they couldn't see me.

'Where is it?' Dad was saying.

'Down at Search Headquarters,' Greer's mum told him.

'In the thylacine cage?'

'No. It's in some sort of crate on the back of a ute.'

'Did you get a look at it?' Dad asked.

'They're not letting anyone go near,' said Mrs Samson.

I realised they were talking about the mother thylacine. Someone must have caught it! That explained why it hadn't been in the Bat Cave when Greer and I visited earlier in the day.

'I'd better get down there,' Dad said.

'What can you do, Al?' she asked.

'I don't know. But maybe I can talk Mr Fergusson into releasing it.'

'Mr Fergusson had to fly back to Sydney on business yesterday,' Greer's mum said.

'Then I'll talk to this Mr Tootell, who caught it,' said Dad following her outside.

After they had gone, I raced back to my bedroom and got dressed. I let myself out the back door, crossed the yard and hurried down the back lane in the direction of the oval.

45 I want to buy the thylacine

There was a big crowd of people there.

They surrounded an old Ford Falcon ute
with South Australian registration plates. It was
parked in the space between the caretaker's shed
and Search Headquarters.

A long rope had been tied to a circle of iron
pickets driven into the ground about ten metres
out from the ute. I supposed this was to stop
anyone getting too close. In the back of the ute
was a large box about the size of a refrigerator
lying on its side.

You couldn't see what was inside it.

Peering through a gap between two thylacine
hunters, I recognised Dad standing inside the
rope talking to a tattered-looking little man with
a bushy white beard. It had to be Mr Tootell.

'It's wrong to take it out of this forest,' Dad was saying. 'It belongs here. It's part of our natural heritage.'

'I caught it! It belongs to me,' said Mr Tootell.

At that moment one of Mr Fergusson's men walked over. It was the same man who had talked to Greer and me earlier in the week.

'Excuse me, sir,' he said to Dad, 'but could you please step back outside the rope?'

And then Dad said a surprising thing.

'I want to buy the thylacine.'

The man just laughed. 'I'm afraid it's not for sale.'

But Dad ignored him. He turned back to Mr Tootell.

'How much do you want for it?' he asked.

The old man shrugged. 'Mr Fergusson is going to pay a million dollars.'

Dad shuffled his feet. I couldn't see his face clearly because the only lights were back at the edge of the oval.

'I'll give you two million,' he said softly.

There were gasps of amazement from around the circle of people watching. And then everyone was dead silent. I'm sure if you'd been standing next to me you would have heard my heart thumping. Dad hasn't got two million dollars, I thought.

He didn't even have two thousand dollars.

Mr Tootell scratched his beard. He must have been thinking the same thing I was.

'Have you got two million dollars?' he asked.

'No I haven't,' Dad admitted. He lowered his head. 'But I might be able to get a loan.'

'You must have a very friendly bank manager,' Mr Fergusson's helper chuckled.

Everybody laughed.

I felt sorry for Dad.

Even I knew that ordinary people like us couldn't borrow two million dollars. It showed me how important it was to return the thylacine to the wild.

Some things are more important than all the money in the world.

Like those two baby thylacines, I suddenly thought. They had to get their mother back. I remembered how bad it was when my mother first went away.

'Don't waste our time, sir,' Mr Fergusson's helper was saying to Dad while I was having all these distracting thoughts. Then he put his arm around Mr Tootell's shoulders.

'I have just phoned Mr Fergusson in Sydney,'
he said, 'and he said to tell you he will be
flying down first thing tomorrow with your one
million dollar reward.'

46 Pop!

That was when I had another one of my
brilliant ideas. Pop! and it was right there in my
head.

   Pop! I knew how I was going to save the
thylacine.

47 How would you like to be famous

I slipped away into the shadows before Dad came out of the crowd, and ran all the way home.

After I let myself into our back yard, I checked to make sure Elvis was safe in his kennel and then hurried inside and jumped into bed still wearing my clothes.

Two minutes later, I heard the front door open and then click softly closed. I lay listening while Dad made himself a cup of tea and watched part of the late News.

I didn't dare close my eyes. If I went to sleep, it was good-bye Mrs Thylacine. Everything depended on my staying awake.

Finally I heard the TV being switched off. Dad rinsed his cup in the kitchen, closed the pantry door, then the loose floorboard outside my door creaked as Dad made his way to the bathroom.

I listened to him brushing his teeth. Now have a gargle, I thought. Sure enough, he gargled. Next the toilet flushed and he washed his hands.

Then the floorboard creaked again and (at last) Dad went to bed.

I waited about half an hour to be sure he was asleep. Then I slipped out of bed and tip-toed out of my room. Being very careful not to step on the creaky floorboard, I made my way down the passage and out the back door. After I got my gumboots on (no socks), I walked over to Elvis' kennel and woke him. 'How would you like to be famous?' I asked him.

Like I wrote at the start, I didn't know there was such a word as infamous. But I was going to learn it pretty soon.

48 A tip

Here is a tip for anyone who plans to paint
stripes on their dog: Don't do it in the dark.

I couldn't risk turning the shed light on
because you can see it from Dad's bedroom.
Instead, I took Elvis around the back of the
shed and painted him on the lawn where there
was a bit of light slanting in from the
streetlight on the corner.

I could tell that Elvis wasn't very happy
about being woken up and painted in the
middle of the night, so I let him lie down while
I worked. At least this time I didn't have to
worry about his wagging tail.

When I finished the first side, I had to wake
him up and get him to roll over so I could do
the other side. It took ages.

I was worried Dad would come out and catch me red-handed. Or should I say black-handed, because almost as much paint was going on me as on Elvis.

At last I was finished. I switched the torch on to see how he looked.

He didn't look too good. The stripes were more like zigzags and there were several leopard-spots as well. Nobody could mistake him for a thylacine. But I figured it didn't matter: in fact it was probably better that the resemblance wasn't exactly perfect—I didn't want him to wind up in Mr Fergusson's zoo.

As we passed the back of Greer's place on our way to the oval, I thought about how she was going to be mad at me again for not letting her be part of my plan.

But I knew it was better this way. There was no sense in both of us getting into trouble.

49 Stumped

It was just after midnight when Elvis and I arrived at the oval.

Everyone had gone home. Or almost everyone. As we approached Mr Tootell's ute from the shady side, I suddenly glimpsed the red glow of a cigarette. Quickly Elvis and I ducked behind the caretaker's shed.

I peered round a corner of the building and saw a shadowy figure standing just inside the rope. With a sinking heart I realised it was one of Mr Fergusson's men guarding the thylacine.

I was stumped. How was I going to get near the ute if a guard was there?

50 Another 'two kid job'

'What are you doing here?' Greer whispered.
'It's the middle of the night!'

Standing in the scratchy rose garden outside her bedroom window, I explained the situation to her.

'Hang on,' she said when I was finished, 'I'll just get dressed.'

Two minutes later the fly-screen popped open and Greer, wearing dark clothes, climbed out over her window sill and dropped lightly down into the garden.

Quickly, she crossed the dark lawn to where Elvis and I were waiting at the corner of their carport.

'I've had an idea,' she whispered. 'The ute is right near the caretaker's shed isn't it?'

I said it was.

'And is the guard wearing a rain coat?' she asked.

I said I didn't think so.

'Perfect!' said Greer.

'What's perfect?' I asked.

'You know how Mum looks after the sprinklers over Christmas when Mr Bennet, the caretaker, goes on holiday?' Greer said. 'Well, she's got her own key to the shed.'

She held up a small silvery object, the key.

'So?' I said. 'The thylacine isn't in the shed.'

'I know that, stupid! But there's other stuff in there.'

'Like what?' I asked.

'Like a hose,' said Greer.

51 A change in the weather

'Okay,' Greer whispered. 'Turn it on.'

I was crouched near the tap just behind the caretaker's shed. Greer was standing next to the building with a hose pointed at an angle up at the sky.

She had screwed a special nozzle onto the end of the hose. When I turned the water on she directed the fine spray up over the roof of the shed.

I peeped around the corner. The water was falling just short of the guard.

'A bit further,' I directed her.

Greer made a little adjustment to the plastic nozzle.

As I watched, the guard stiffened and suddenly looked round. For a horrible moment,

I thought he had heard us. But then he looked up at the sky and put one hand out, palm upwards, like people do when it's starting to rain. He shook his head and swore softly.

Then he swung round and walked quickly away in the direction of Search Headquarters.

'It worked,' I told Greer. 'Make sure Elvis isn't asleep.'

Then I darted out from behind the shed and ran flat out over to the ute.

52 Operation Elvis

A low growl came from inside the wooden crate as I climbed up onto the back of the ute.

'It's okay,' I whispered. 'I've come to rescue you.'

I know it's pretty dumb to talk to animals. Our words are just noises to them. But I reckon they know from the tone of your voice whether you're friendly or not. And I think it's possible, too, that you can communicate with them if there's something you really want them to understand.

So I talked softly to the thylacine the whole time I worked to untie the big triple knot in the rope that held the door of the crate closed.

I told her about her babies, how Greer and I had gone to see them, and that they were okay.

I told her I was sorry about what civilisation had done to the forests she lived in and to all the other thylacines that had been killed by people who didn't know any better.

I said I was sorry that she had been locked up like this; I said there were greedy people in the world who cared only about money; but I said there were lots of good people too! People like my dad who were working to save the forests that were left and the animals who lived there.

And the last thing I told her, before the door came open, was to take her babies out of the Bat Cave and go off somewhere so far from civilisation that no humans would ever go there.

I know she understood me, because when the door finally swung open and the thylacine stepped out onto the lowered tailgate of the ute, she paused for a moment and looked at me.

Only ten centimetres separated us.

Even in the dark I saw the calmness in her eyes.

She was a wild animal, but she wasn't afraid of me. And it's funny, I wasn't afraid of her either. We were the same, just two living things whose lives touched for that brief moment in time.

And then she leapt down off the back of the ute and was gone.

I knew I would never set eyes on her again.

I ran back to the shed.

'Is Elvis ready?' I asked.

Greer brought him out from the shed and handed me his lead. I hurried with him back to the ute and helped him climb up onto the tailgate. Then I removed his collar, whispered good night, and closed him inside the wooden crate.

I had just re-tied the knot and rushed back to the shed when the guard came back wearing a bright yellow raincoat.

'Won't he be surprised in the morning,' Greer said, 'when he discovers he's been up all night guarding a painted dog?'

53 Something better

I guess you know the rest of the story.

They found Elvis in Mr Tootell's cage next morning and worked out the whole thing was a hoax.

Obviously there wasn't a thylacine living in the forest near Daffodil after all.

All along it was just a dog painted to look like one.

You probably saw me and Elvis on TV, and in all the newspapers.

Tim Chambers, The Boy Who Fooled The Whole World Into Thinking The Thylacine Was Not Really Extinct

Most people were pretty sporting about it. Australians like a good joke.

Mr Fergusson came to see me next day (when they brought Elvis back) and said if ever I was in Sydney, he would be only too happy to put me up in his empty thylacine cage.

He winked when he said that.

Dad invited him to stay for lunch.

Over a big feed of fish and chips, Dad told him about his idea to make a large section of the forest near Daffodil into a reserve for native animals.

Dad said a good name for it would be— *Fergusson Wildlife Reserve*.

Mr Fergusson agreed it was a good idea and he wrote out a cheque for a million dollars to help set it up.

Do you suppose Dad suspects something?

He wasn't at all upset when he found out about my prank. And he said something strange after Mr Fergusson left too.

'It's funny,' he said, 'but in a way Mr Fergusson got what he wanted.'

'What do you mean?' I asked.

Dad smiled. 'Well! All along he wanted to put the thylacine behind wire, didn't he?'

Mr Tootell stayed in Daffodil after all the other thylacine hunters left. He liked the look of the place and decided to do some prospecting while he was in the area. When he took his metal-detector into the Bat Cave, he didn't find any sign of thylacines.

What he did find though was a gold nugget about the size of a football buried just under the tunnel floor.

'Just think,' Greer said, 'we must have walked right over it!'

'But we found something better,' I said.

54 Infamous

That Monday at the start of English, Mr Gilbert asked me what it was like being famous.

I told him I wasn't famous. I was *infamous*.

He nodded. 'That's very astute of you Tim, and...' he continued, 'as a special English assignment, I want you to write the full story of how you became infamous.'

I've got until the end of term to write it.

Yesterday, Mr Gilbert asked me how it was coming along. Okay, I said. He doesn't know I've already finished.

The **full** story, that is. **This** one.

The one I'll write for Mr Gilbert will be much shorter; I'll leave lots of bits out, because I know Mr Gilbert will never be able to keep my secret.

I hope you can.

Check out these mind-tickling adventures by Justin D'Ath...

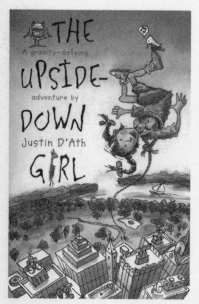

THE
A gravity-defying
UPSIDE-
adventure by
DOWN
Justin D'Ath
GIRL

Justin D'Ath
ASTRID
SPARK,
fixologist
The girl with the
incredible magnetic
fingers

pictures by Terry Denton

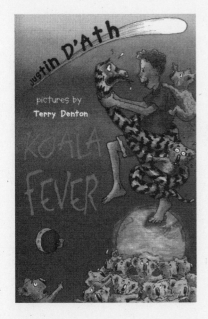

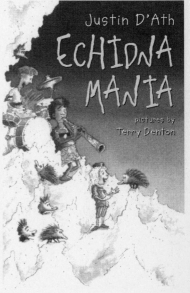